Richard Edwards was born in Tonbridge, Kent, and studied English and American literature at Warwick University. Since then he has lived in Italy, France and Spain. The author of some 20 picture books and books of poetry for children, his most recent titles include *Amazing Animal Alphabet* and *Nonsense Nursery Rhymes*, *Big ABC Book* and *Little ABC Book* (all OUP); *Moon Frog* and *Moles Can Dance* (Walker); *You're Safe Now, Waterdog* (Orion); and *Ten Tall Oaktrees* (Red Fox).

Susan Winter was born in South Africa and graduated from Natal University, before becoming a social worker, first in South Africa and later in London. After the birth of her second child, she studied illustration at Chelsea School of Art and began a new career as a freelance illustrator of children's books. Her previous titles include *Henry's Baby* and *The Bear That Went to Ballet* (DK); the *Winchelsea Trilogy* and *The Ghost Watchers* (Hodder and Stoughton); *Calling All Toddlers* and *Toddler Times* (Orion); and *Nicky and the Twins* (Harper Collins). Among her titles for Frances Lincoln are *Acker Backa Boo!* by Opal Dunn. Susan lives in West London.

Richard Edwards and Susan Winter have previously collaborated on another Copycub story: *Copy Me, Copycub*.

To Francesca and Charlotte – *S.W.*

First published in Great Britain in 2001 by
Frances Lincoln Limited, 4 Torriano Mews,
Torriano Avenue, London NW5 2RZ

First paperback edition 2002

British Library Cataloguing in Publication Data
available on request

ISBN 0-7112-1760-2 hb
ISBN 0-7112-1860-9 pb

Printed in Singapore

9 8 7 6 5 4 3 2

Where Are You Hiding, Copycub?

Richard Edwards

Illustrated by Susan Winter

FRANCES LINCOLN

Copycub was a young bear who loved playing games. His favourite game was hiding, but he could never think of a good enough place, and his mother always found him.

In the spring the bears woke up from their long winter's sleep.
Copycub's mother stretched. Copycub stretched.
Copycub's mother scratched. Copycub scratched.
Then he crept to hide in a corner of the bearcave.

"Can't find me here!" he called.
"Oh, yes I can," said his mother.
She tiptoed across the cave, reached into the shadows and lifted the small bear high above her head.
"Got you, little Copycub!"

When summer came to the north woods, the bears spent all day outside in the sunshine.

"Can't find me here!" called Copycub, hiding in the bushes.

"Oh, yes I can," replied his mother. And she lolloped through the trees, running straight to the young bear's hiding place.

"Got you again!" she said, kissing him on the nose.

In autumn all the bears gathered at the big river to fish for salmon.

"Can't find me here!" called Copycub, hiding behind the sticks
of a beaver dam.

But his mother splashed through the water and scooped him up.

"Oh, yes I can, my little furry fish!"

One afternoon, while the bears were exploring deep in the woods, Copycub thought of a really good place to hide. When his mother wasn't looking he slipped away, ran down to a stream and climbed the hill on the other side until he came to a hollow tree.

With a squeeze and a wriggle, he pushed inside.

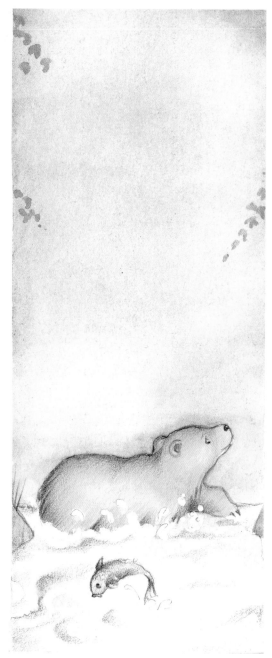

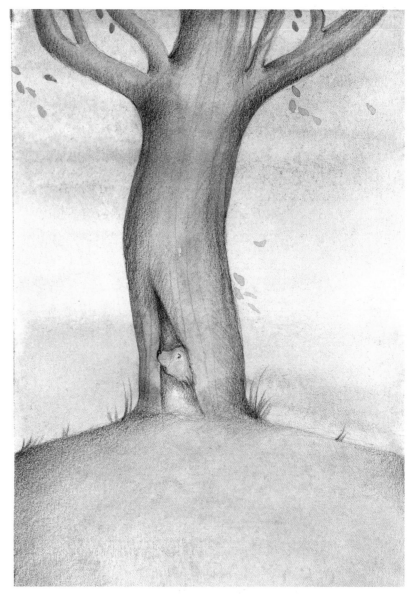

"Can't find me here!" called Copycub. There was no reply.

"Can't find me here!" he called again, a little louder. Again there was no reply.

"Can't find me here!" he shouted at the top of his voice.
But the only answer was the swish of the wind through
the tree-tops.

Copycub felt very alone. He squeezed out of the hollow tree
and began to run back the way he had come.

But he took the wrong path, and was soon completely lost
in the darkening woods.

He ran this way. He ran that way. He didn't know what to do.

Copycub sat down and shivered.

Night was falling. An owl hooted, and the woods made sudden noises as a leaf fell, or a twig scraped, or a tree groaned in the wind.

Then Copycub heard a louder noise: a slow and heavy rustling coming steadily towards him. He crawled behind a fallen log and hid, making himself as small as he could and covering his eyes with his paws.

"Can't find me here!" he whispered.

"Oh, yes I can."
It was his mother's voice. Copycub was so happy to see her!

He jumped up and ran
into her arms.
  "I knew you'd find me,"
he said. "I knew you would."

When they were back in the bearcave, Copycub's mother told him never to run off on his own again.

"I won't," said Copycub. "I promise."

And he snuggled up close to his mother's warm side. He was very tired.

"But if I get lost, will you always come to find me?" he asked.

"Always," said his mother quietly.

"Always, always?"

"Always, always."

Copycub yawned.

"Always, always...?"

He meant to say it three times, but after the second time he fell asleep.

So his mother said it for him:

"Always, Copycub."

MORE TITLES AVAILABLE IN PAPERBACK
FROM FRANCES LINCOLN

Chimp and Zee
Catherine and Laurence Anholt

Up jumps Chimp. Up jumps Zee. "Ha, ha, ha!" "Hee, hee, hee!"
Meet Chimp and Zee, the mischievous monkey twins and follow them
on an exciting adventure through Jungletown and beyond!

Suitable for Nursery and Early Years Education and for National Curriculum English – Reading, Key Stage 1
Scottish Guidelines English Language – Reading, Level A

ISBN 0-7112-1897-8 £6.99

I Have Feelings
Jana Novotny Hunter
Illustrated by Sue Porter

Everybody has feelings – especially me and you!
Small children will fall in love with the adorable star of *I Have Feelings!* –
an essential book for learning to express your emotions.

Suitable for Nursery and Early Years Education
Scottish Guidelines English Language – Reading, Level A

ISBN 0-7112-1734-3 £5.99

Noko and the Night Monster
Fiona Moodie

Takadu the Aardvark and Noko the Porcupine have a wonderful life together,
cooking, playing and making up songs. But every bedtime Takadu shivers and shakes
because he's afraid of the Night Monster. Perfect for children who are afraid
of the dark, this is a delightful and reassuring story.

Suitable for Nursery and Early Years Education and for National Curriculum English – Reading, Key Stage 1
Scottish Guidelines English Language – Reading, Level A

ISBN 0-7112-1826-9 £5.99

Frances Lincoln titles are available from all good bookshops.
Prices are correct at time of publication, but may be subject to change.